Lily
Leads
the Way

To Arno, my sailing partner
MP

For Bill and Tom,
who helped me navigate new waters
MM

First edition 2022. Library of Congress Catalog Card Number pending. ISBN 978-1-5362-1403-1.
This book was typeset in Dolly. The illustrations were done in oil on illustration board.
Candlewick Press, 99 Dover Street, Somerville, Massachusetts 02144. www.candlewick.com.
Printed in Humen, Dongguan, China. 22 23 24 25 26 27 APS 10 9 8 7 6 5 4 3 2 1

Lily Leads the Way

MARGI PREUS

illustrated by MATT MYERS

CANDLEWICK PRESS

Today is a big day for Lily the little sailboat.
A fleet of grand old tall ships is coming to visit.
Lily wants to go out on the lake to greet them.

With decks scrubbed, lines coiled, brass gleaming, flags flying,
and sails puffed out proudly, she glides from the harbor toward the lake.

At the harbor entrance is a bridge that goes up to let ships
pass under, then down to let cars go across. Even though Lily
is small, her mast is tall, and the bridge must go up to let her
pass under. Lily blows her horn to ask the bridge to lift.

"Meee-me? Meee-me?"

But a big ore boat blasts its horn much louder:

"OOHHH-pen.
OOHHH-pen."

The bridge answers:

"OOOHHH-kay. OOOHHH-kay."

The bridge goes up, up, up. Lily hurries toward it.

"MOOOOVE aside!" the big ship blasts at Lily. "I've got a bellyful of iron ore, and I can't stop or turn very fast. Better MOOOVE!"
Lily scoots away, rocking unsteadily in the big ship's waves.

The thousand-footer—almost as long as the ship canal—passes under the bridge.
Then the bridge goes down, down, down.

Now is it Lily's turn?

She blows her horn again.

"Meee-me?
Meee-me?"

But out on the lake, a big seagoing vessel lets out a loud, low blast of its horn:

"oOHHH-pen. OOHHH-pen."

And the bridge answers:

"oOOHHH-kay. OOOHHH-kay."

The bridge goes up, up, up.
The "saltie" passes under.
"Watch out, little boat," he booms as Lily tries to squeeze past.
"I've come all the way across the ocean—I'm not stopping now!"

Lily lurches over the big ship's wake.

A tugboat honks, "Outta my way!"

Flustered, Lily turns the wrong direction, swaying and bobbing.

When a coast guard cutter chugs by,
its wake heels Lily over!

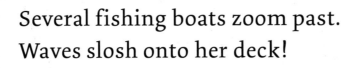

Several fishing boats zoom past.
Waves slosh onto her deck!

But she rights herself and at the very last minute slips under the bridge just before it goes down again.

And here they come! Grand old granddaddies and grandmamas.
Tall ships. Big ships. With sails a-brimming and flags a-flying.

Lily's sails flutter with excitement as she floats out to meet them.

There's a sloop,

a schooner,

a brig,

a barque,

and a barquentine, all sailing
toward the harbor.

Silently sailing.

No blast of horns.

Not even a
tootley-toot.

Who will tell the bridge to open?
They are very tall ships with very tall masts.
The bridge will have to lift up up up up up
for the ships to fit under.

Lily trims her sails and
tacks toward the bridge.
She toots her horn:

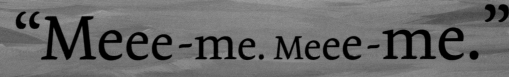
"Meee-me. Meee-me."

The tall ships glide closer.
The bridge does not go up.

Lily toots as loud as she can.

"MEEE — ME! MEEE — ME!"

She turns circles. She flaps her sails.
What can she do to make the bridge go up?

"OH, PLEEAASE — please!"
"PLEEAASE — please!"

And the bridge answers:

"OOOHHH—kay. OOOHHH—kay."

The bridge goes up, up, up up up up!
The majestic ships—
a sloop,
a schooner,
a brig,
a barque, and
a barquentine—
pass under.

At the front of the procession, with her decks scrubbed, lines coiled, brass gleaming, flags flying, and sails puffed out proudly, Lily leads the way.

AUTHOR'S NOTE

There are many different kinds of bridges. Some are very long, like the Golden Gate Bridge in San Francisco and the one across Lake Pontchartrain in Louisiana. Some are very high, like the one over the Royal Gorge in Colorado and the Liuguanghe Bridge in Guizhou, China, which is 1,000 feet (305 meters) high.

Some bridges allow ships to pass through, under, or even over them. Drawbridges lift up on one end. Folding bridges collapse together horizontally. A bascule bridge opens in the middle. A retractable or thrust bridge pulls open to one side, and a submersible bridge goes down, underwater, to allow boats to pass over.

The bridge in this story is a lift bridge. Its roadway is raised to let ships pass under. Although there are other lift bridges, there are only two like this particular bridge. One is located in Rouen, France. The one in this story is called the Aerial Lift Bridge and is located at the westernmost end of the Great Lakes, on the tip of the nose on the wolf's head that is the shape of Lake Superior. It has a span of 386 feet (118 meters) and weighs 900 tons (816 metric tons). The bridge can be raised to its full height of 135 feet (41 meters) in about a minute. It is raised about five thousand times per year. In the busy summer season, it averages twenty-six lifts per day.

My husband and I used to have a sailboat like Lily—little but with a tall mast. In order to sail onto the lake from the harbor, we had to wait for the bridge to open, and we only had a tiny horn that we blew to let the bridge know that we'd like it lifted. But our boat was so small and our horn so pathetic and some of the ships that passed by were so big that we didn't dare squeeze by when they were in the ship canal. Sometimes it seemed like a long wait to get out, although we never waited as long as poor Lily does in this story.

Nowadays ships and larger boats use radios to communicate with the bridge, and smaller craft have to wait for the half-hour raising of the bridge to go in and out. Before radios were the preferred method of communication, LOONNGG—short, LOONNGG—short meant "open the bridge" and the same from the bridge served as an acknowledgment. Today vessels often blast a LOONNGG—short, short, and the bridge will respond in kind. This is a kind of friendly "thank you" and "you're welcome," so it's not too hard to imagine that a polite "PLEEAASE—please" might be just the ticket to get the bridge to open.